W9-BSF-440

TiNA and the PeNGUiN

To mom and dad, with much love from your eldest penguin — H.D.

To Yves, my favorite penguin — M.L.

Text © 2002 Heather Dyer
Illustrations © 2002 Mireille Levert

Kids Can Press acknowledges the financial support of the Ontario Arts Council, the Canada Council for the Arts and the Government of Canada, through the BPIDP, for our publishing activity.

Published in Canada by
Kids Can Press Ltd.
29 Birch Avenue
Toronto, ON M4V 1E2

Published in the U.S. by
Kids Can Press Ltd.
2250 Military Road
Tonawanda, NY 14150

www.kidscanpress.com

The artwork in this book was rendered in watercolor and gouache. The text is set in Celeste.

Edited by Debbie Rogosin
Designed by Karen Powers
Printed in Hong Kong, China, by Wing King Tong Co. Ltd.

This book is smyth sewn casebound.

CM 02 0 9 8 7 6 5 4 3 2 1

National Library of Canada Cataloguing in Publication Data

Dyer, Heather, 1970–
    Tina and the penguin

ISBN 1-55074-947-1

1. Penguins — Juvenile fiction. I. Levert, Mireille. II. Title.

PS8557.Y476T55 2002   jC813'.6   C2001-903440-7
PZ7.D976Ti 2002

Kids Can Press is a Corus™ Entertainment company

TiNA aNd the PENGUiN

Written by Heather Dyer
Illustrated by Mireille Levert

Kids Can Press

"You in the pink beret!"
cried the zookeeper. "Hurry up!"

"Coming," said Tina, but she hung back a moment
longer to look at the penguins.

"Back to the bus!" cried the keeper.

Tina turned to follow the rest of the class, but as she
did something landed on the concrete behind her with a
wet *whump*. Tina looked around. A penguin had leaped
right out of the enclosure and was lying flat on his
belly! He pedaled his feet and flapped his wings to
right himself, and then stood there looking at her.

"Are you all right?" asked Tina.

The penguin blinked.

"Everyone back to the bus!" yelled the keeper. Tina turned to go but then she heard a sound. *Schlep, schlep.* She looked around. The penguin stood there innocently, but as soon as Tina turned her back she heard the sound of wet footsteps again. *Schlep, schlep.* The penguin was following her.

Tina sighed. "They'll never let you out," she said. The penguin just looked at her. "I'd like to help," she said. "But what can I do?"

Then she had an idea. "Come on then," said Tina, "quick." And she took off her coat and held it out. The penguin shuffled over, turned his back and slipped his wings into the sleeves. Tina buttoned the coat up around his neck and stood back to look at him.

"You've got a very small head," said Tina. "And such a big nose." She thought for a moment and then took off her pink beret and put it on the penguin. "There," she said. "Follow me." She took the penguin by the sleeve and set off after the rest of the class.

"You in the pink beret," said the keeper, slapping the penguin on the back. "We're always waiting for you!"

Tina and the penguin hurried to catch up with the others.

"Who's your friend?" asked Stephanie when they got back on the bus.

"Shhh ..." whispered Tina. "He's a penguin."

"He's dripping on the seat," said Stephanie.

"I'm taking him home," whispered Tina. "Don't tell."

"Home?" exclaimed Stephanie. "You'll never get to Antarctica and back before bedtime — even if your dad takes you."

"Not *his* home," hissed Tina. "*Mine.*" They stared at the penguin, who looked up at them both and blinked.

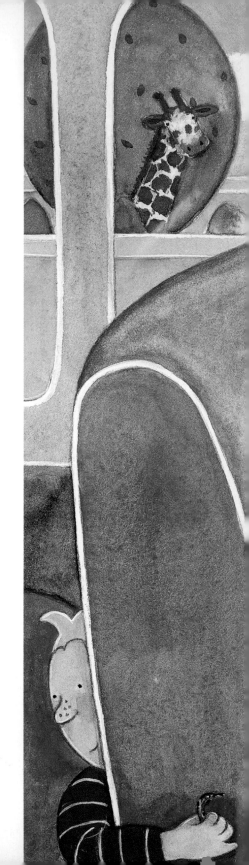

While her parents were cooking dinner, Tina smuggled the penguin upstairs.

"Here we are!" she said proudly, opening her bedroom door. "Your new home."

The penguin just stood there.

"In you go," said Tina.

The penguin didn't move.

"Dinner's ready!" called Tina's mother.

Tina gave the penguin a little push. "Go on!" she said, and she shut the door.

When Tina went up to bed, she found her window wide open. The room was freezing cold, but the penguin was sitting on the bed among Tina's stuffed toys, fanning himself to keep cool. Tina sighed, put on her nightie and a thick pair of socks, got out her woolly hat and climbed into bed.

Soon Tina's mother came in to say good night. "Brrrrr!" she said, and she went to close the window.

"It's okay!" cried Tina. "Leave it open!" She kicked off her socks, flung back the duvet and flapped her nightie up and down. "I'm boiling!" she said.

"Are you feeling all right?" asked her mother, putting her hand on Tina's forehead.

"Yes," said Tina. "I'm just hot."

Then Tina's mother spotted the penguin. "Where did you get that penguin?" she asked.

"What penguin?" said Tina.

"That stuffed toy on your bed."

"Oh, *that* penguin," said Tina. "I got him at the zoo."

As soon as her mother had gone, Tina breathed a sigh of relief. She put her socks back on, pulled her woolly hat down over her ears and wriggled under the duvet.

"Good night," Tina said in a muffled voice.

There was no reply.

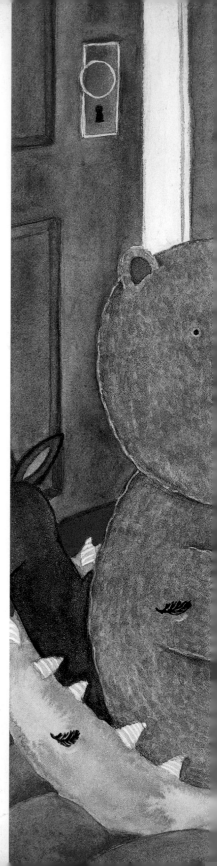

The next morning, Tina opened a can of sardines for the penguin and brought him a glass of water. She gave him her *Antarctic Wildlife* picture book and went off to school.

But in class, Tina couldn't concentrate at all. She kept thinking about the penguin.

At last the bell rang. Tina ran all the way home, went straight to her room, flung open the door and was greeted by a flurry of feathers.

"Uh-oh," she said.

Tina's mother had been in to shut the window, and in the warmth of Tina's bedroom the penguin had begun to molt. Downy feathers had settled over everything like snowflakes and were piled up in drifts in the corners of the room. The penguin was reclining limply in the arms of Tina's largest teddy. Tina opened the window and ran here and there catching up the feathers and stuffing them into her sock drawer before her mother saw them.

"There's a funny fishy smell in your room," remarked Tina's mother at dinner.

"That's strange," said Tina.

"And I think your duvet's got a hole in it," said her mother. "Either that or one of your toys is losing its stuffing."

Tina noticed a feather in her mother's hair but said nothing.

"How's the penguin?" asked Stephanie at school the next day.

"Not good," said Tina with a sigh. "His feathers are falling out."

"Maybe it's normal," said Stephanie.

Tina wasn't so sure.

When Tina got home from school, she found the refrigerator door wide open and the penguin sitting on the middle shelf next to the milk. There were footprints in the butter and feathers in the jam.

"What are you doing in there?" Tina cried. "Get back to my room!" She hurried the penguin upstairs and then went to clean up the mess before her mother came home from work.

As a special treat, Tina let the penguin share her bath that evening. But the penguin liked the water freezing cold and full of ice cubes. Tina sat shivering, while the penguin splashed about. He made such a noise that Tina's mother rapped on the door and called, "Are you all right in there?"

"Fine!" yelled Tina.

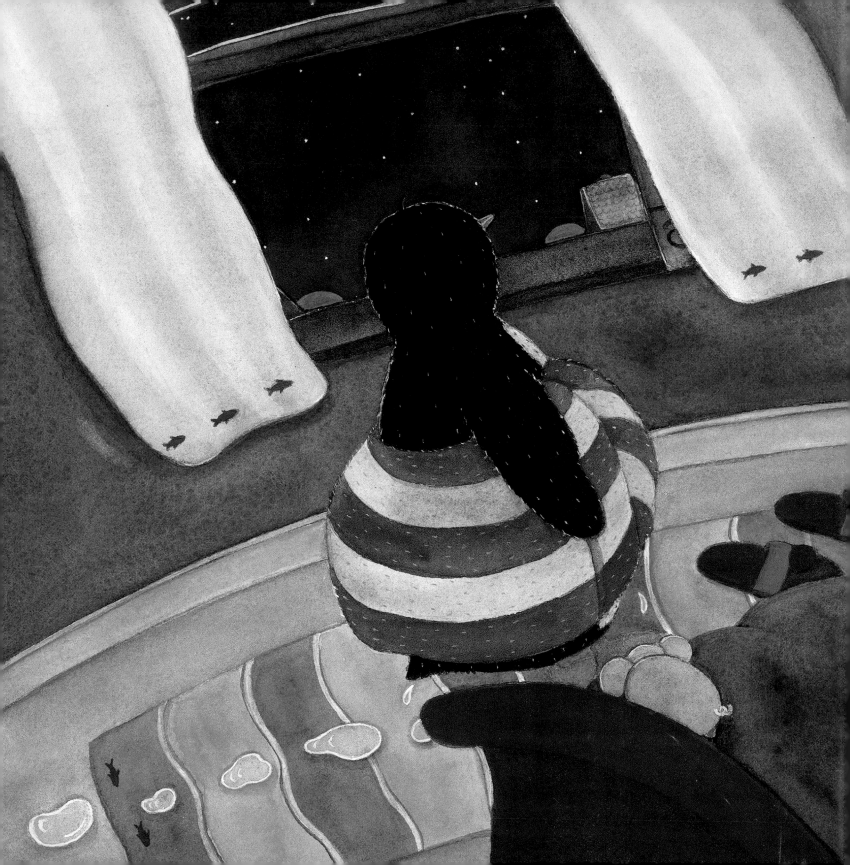

They hurried back to Tina's room swaddled in towels, the penguin schlepping along behind and leaving large wet footprints on the carpet. Tina climbed into bed and pulled on her hat. She was blue with cold.

"I don't think this is working out," she said, her teeth chattering.

The penguin made no reply, but long after Tina had fallen asleep he remained standing at the open window, looking at the stars.

The next morning when Tina woke up, the penguin was gone. Tina tossed her stuffed toys onto the floor, but the penguin was not among them. All that remained were a few feathers blowing across the carpet in the draft from the open window.

Tina put her head out and looked down the street, but there was no sign of the penguin. She closed the window and raced downstairs.

"What about breakfast?" called her mother, as Tina rushed outside in her nightie.

Tina looked in every yard, but there was no sign of the penguin. The streets were quiet, and there was no one about except the letter carrier.

"Did you see a penguin?" Tina asked.

"Penguin?" he said. "Certainly not! I've seen no one this morning except a small guy in a pink beret hitching out of town."

"Too bad about the penguin," said Stephanie when she heard.

Tina sighed. "Maybe it's for the best," she said.

"Where do you think he went?" asked Stephanie.

"I don't know," said Tina. "I just hope he found a good home."

One evening a few weeks later, Tina's father was watching a program about Antarctica.

"Look at all those penguins," he said. "What a noise they're making!"

"Welcome to Antarctica!" shouted the announcer. He was standing in the middle of an enormous penguin colony. The penguins were crowded close together and were making a tremendous racket. "Extreme conditions ..." yelled the man above the noise, "but these birds are right at home!"

"Remarkable," said Tina's father.

"What an awful place to live!" said Tina's mother with a shiver. "So cold!"

"Oh, I don't know," said Tina. "I think that's the way they like it." Then she noticed something. Surely not ... It couldn't be ... Tina took a closer look. Then she smiled.

One of the penguins was wearing a pink beret.